Michelle Taylor grew up in Darwin and Brisbane. She has lived in Suffolk, Glasgow, London and the island of Madeira in Portugal. She has been writing and publishing for over twenty years. Michelle has a degree in occupational therapy with many years experience helping people navigate their mental and emotional health. She also has a Master of Arts in which she researched how the role of monsters in stories can empower children and manage fears. Michelle particularly enjoys taking poetry to young audiences.

www.mudanca.com.au

Also by Michelle Taylor

If the World Belonged to Dogs

If Bees Rode Shiny Bicycles

The Angel of Barbican High

100 ways to fly

Michelle Taylor

First published 2019 by University of Queensland Press
PO Box 6042, St Lucia, Queensland 4067 Australia

uqp.com.au
uqp@uqp.uq.edu.au

Cover design by Jo Hunt
Cover illustrations: Ladybug: nimna365/Shutterstock; Kite: Fuga/Shutterstock;
Paper Plane: Mr Thanakorn Kotpootorn/Shutterstock
Author photograph by Benjamin Dougherty
Typeset in 13/19 pt Adobe Garamond Pro by Post Pre-press Group, Brisbane
Printed in Australia by McPherson's Printing Group

The University of Queensland Press is supported by the Queensland Government through Arts Queensland.

Australia Council for the Arts

The University of Queensland Press is assisted by the Australian Government through the Australia Council, its arts funding and advisory body.

ISBN 978 0 7022 6250 0 (pbk)
ISBN 978 0 7022 6240 1 (epdf)
ISBN 978 0 7022 6241 8 (epub)
ISBN 978 0 7022 6242 5 (kindle)

A catalogue record for this book is available from the National Library of Australia.

University of Queensland Press uses papers that are natural, renewable and recyclable products made from wood grown in well-managed forests. The logging and manufacturing processes conform to the environmental regulations of the country of origin.

For the biggest and the littlest –

my dad, Ross
&
my daughter, Sappho

Contents

Poems about the amazing creatures found in language

Found

I dropped my page
in a puddle –
and it became
a poem.

Thesaurus

There is no synonym.
There is no chorus.
Indeed there is no other way
to say the word THESAURUS.

The word 'thesaurus' comes from a Greek word that means a storehouse of precious items, or a treasure.

What's in a Few Words

There's an owl in my vowel.
You can be in my verb.

There's an ant in consonant,
but nun in noun.

There's ten in a sentence,
but it's lost in the fullstop.

You'll find your self on a shelf
and love in a novel.

There's a toy in your story
and a peach in each chapter.

You'll see me in a poem
and in every rhyme.

And if you read a bit more
into all you've heard,

you may just find a sword
hidden in these words.

Catch

Catch a cold
Catch a name
Catch some ZZZs
Catch a plane

Catch the breeze
Catch a ball
Catch a kiss
Catch your fall

Catch a movie
Catch the news
Catch the score
Catch 22

Catch the leader
Catch a train
Catch the light
Catch the rain

Catch your toe
Catch your breath
Catch some rays
Catch your death

Catch a ride
Catch a fish
Catch you later
Catch your wish

Is Was Will

Was is a wonderful word,
so self-assured,
so wise, so worldly,
always aware
of where it's been,
what it's done
and heard and seen,

whereas *Will*
is a wavering word,
forever wondering
about when and what
and where and how,
never certain of the end,
waiting for what's beyond
the bend
that leads to now,

but *Is* is not worried
about then and when.
Is was *Will*
but in an instant is *Was.*
Time is its personal friend
for *Is* is the start and the end
again and again and again.

The Weight of a Word

Which word weighs more?

lump or *sum*
thump or *run*
bump or *hum*

Each has 'u' at its heart.

Some words are made of breath.
Some words are made of stone.

Listen, weigh them carefully,
to make music for your poem.

Ten Syllables for All Sorts of Things

BO

sweaty clothes
block your nose
breathe through your mouth

Nostrils

cave of hidden
treasures – don't
dig too deep

Late

no breakfast
wrong socks
long red lights
no lunch!

Exams

sweat   drips
gone blank   blank
deep breath
remember

Embarrassment

bright red face
banging heart
squeaky voice
RUN!

Holidays

late-night movies
no homework
no worries

Chocolate Box

hard or soft?
light or dark?
wrong choice again!

Doggy Bottom Burp

half-asleep
its silent creep
chokes the room

Doggerel

Doggone
Hot dog
Dog-day afternoon
Dog Star
Dog-leg
Doggy doos

Dog's body
Dog-eared
Gone to the dogs
Dog paddle
Doggedness
Dog-eat-dog

x

An ‘x’ can be …

a kiss
a cross
a little
a lot

variable
letter
number
noun

a star
a symbol
lost
and found

first aid
graphed plot
buried treasure
marks the spot

a saltire
a stitch
signature
crucifix

chromosome
one for men
two for women
Roman ten

cardinal points
multiplication
intersection
a generation

After a circle an 'x' is one of the first symbols drawn by children around the world.

I Do and I Don't

I could
but I shouldn't

I would
but I couldn't

I can't
but I should

I can
but I won't

I need
but I want

I do
and I don't

I didn't
but I would

I haven't
but I should

I can
and I might

I will
and I won't

I have
and I haven't

I do
and I don't

Names

cannot hurt you
but they may keep you safe.

They are sounds and silence,
letters on a page;

consonants and vowels,
a noise or two moving through

your lips and lungs,
across teeth and tongues

to vanish into air
or fall between cracks in the path.

To be left behind in places
or remembered as faces,

handed down through families
and their trees,

passed around with meals,
shouted across fields,

telling you when it's your turn,
whether you lost or won.

The reason to open the door
or to keep you up all night.

They are a land, a time,
a language, a season,

a homecoming, a hug,
somewhere to cry,

the *Hello*, the *Goodbye*
that could change your life.

Little Poem Made of Questions

after Pablo Neruda

Is the essential ingredient in marshmallows
air or the colour pink?

Would you measure laughter
in bananas or nostrils?

Will I hear better in the dark
if I wear my glasses?

Would all the books in the world
stretch to the moon, and back?

Is there a place where the stars
can fall asleep?

Is there a muscle that stretches
when I have a good idea?

What uses the most energy –
a smile or a frown?

When I cry, is it just my eyes
that fill with tears or my whole body?

Is hope the colour of oranges
or lemons?

When the branch wakes up
will it become the stick insect?

How many little princes wait
in the slime of the tadpole pond?

Are all the birds singing
because someone baked me a cake?

If butterflies could write poetry
what would their poems look like?

Where did the weeping paperbark
learn to cry?

Why don't they make computers
that let us smell the flowers?

Which is longer – an hour on Sunday
or a minute on Monday?

If the colour orange runs out
how will we make sunsets?

Will the frog in my letterbox
read the postcards?

Is there a bridge I can cross
to travel safely to morning?

If I were smarter
would I ask more or fewer questions?

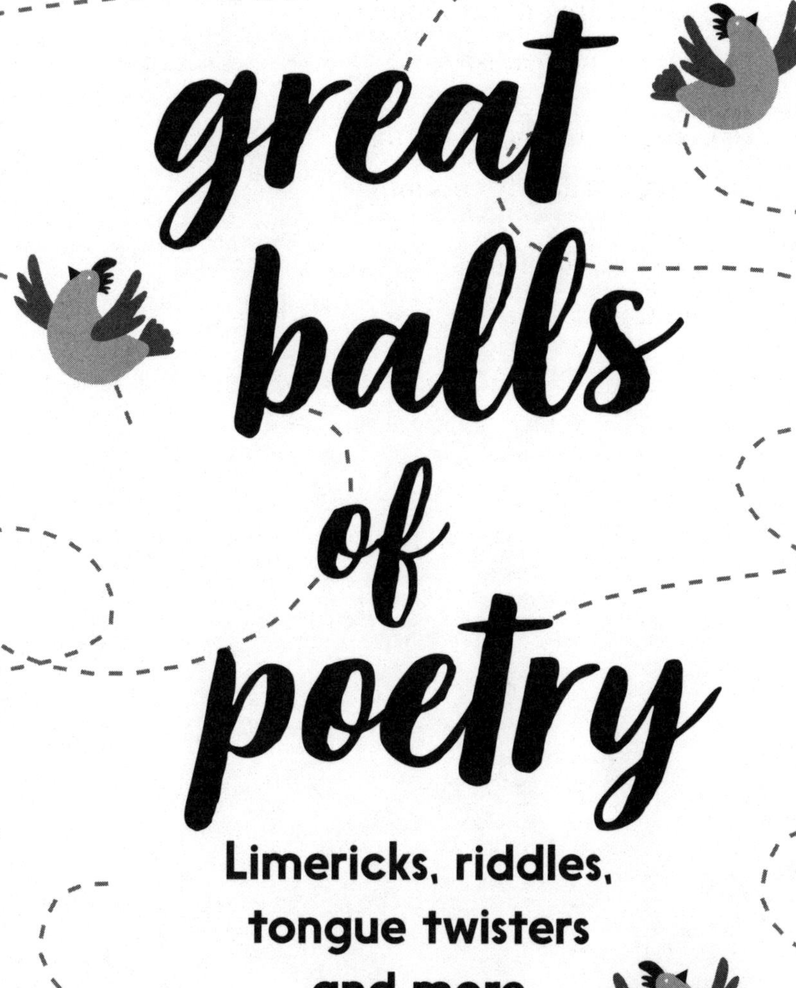

Limericks, riddles, tongue twisters and more

The Lamington Thief

Beware of the Lamington Thief
with chocolate on his teeth.
He will say, *I took none* –
but a coconut crumb
can alert you to his deceit.

Limerick for a Lousy Day

For days when the world does not entice,
when you need a friend, but you don't want
 advice,
you may find that a poem
helps you feel less alone.
I'm sorry I can't be more precise.

From Hair to Hong Kong

A tickly prickly pear
decided to grow its hair.
Its locks grew so long
they stretched to Hong Kong
and it saved all its friends the airfare.

Human hair grows about fifteen centimetres per year.

Chickety Wickety Sense

A rickety pickety fence
made the tightrope walker tense.
She wobbled and shook,
then flew – like a chook.
What chickety wickety sense!

Rusty Limerick

Greedy, ravenous rust
will turn your steel to dust.
Add oxygen, add water
and salt to nature's mortar.
Then watch it all combust!

Shauna and Shaun

Shauna and Shaun share a suitcase.
So shall they also share their sets of
sheets, shirts, shorts, skirts, shoes and socks?

Three Small Sisters

If three small sisters
swapped seven tongue twisters
for seven short songs
to sing at sing-a-longs,
which seven songs
should those three small sisters sing?

Five One-liners

Fondu

Cheese – with no skeleton!

Louvres

The way a window winks.

Smoothie

The next best thing to inhaling fruit!

Happiness

Sunlight skipping across the table.

Breath

Little string that connects me to the earth.

Sunflower

A bright clock within the flower
measures the sun in every hour.

Sunflowers follow the sun across the sky during the day. This movement is called heliotropism.

Seven Riddles

What am I?

One

Soft landing for my tears,
little bed to rest my fears.
With it, I share not just sleep,
for I know only it can keep
each secret that it hears.

Two

I am as large and as small as the air,
maker of static for your hair.
I view the world from below your knees
and from high above the trees,
but I cannot survive a tear.

Three

I have skin, but I do not wash.
I am hard, but I also squash.
My colours are brown, yellow, green.
I come on my own or as part of a team,
the complete all-round no-nonsense nosh.

Four

You hold me, yet cannot touch me,
outline of my memory
in silver, black, gold.
Within your arms I won't grow old.
Though not a mirror, you still reflect me.

Five

Short and long,
the riddle and the song.
I don't own you, yet you are mine.
Not a shape, yet made of lines,
something to carry my whole life long.

Six

Stays for a week, but never years.
Brings warmth, pleasure, pain, tears.
If you see the sky, it might visit you,
but its colour is pink, never blue.
The damage lasts after it disappears.

Seven

Made of waves, but it's not the sea;
a name, a call, a song, a decree.
It scales cliffs in a single bounce,
but it isn't alive and cannot pounce.
When you are lost, set it free.

- -

You can find the answers to the riddles on page 135.

Poems about school, sport and shrinking seasons

Work

Waits for me
at the foot of my bed.
I dare not open my eyes today,
I dare not lift my head,
for once it sees me stirring
it owns the day ahead.

Tuck-shop

Two syllables,
two words,

mean rather little
when kept apart,

but when joined together
break into a paper-bag smile!

Eating in Class – A WARNING

If you hide your half-chewed bubblegum under
your chair for later,
if you have two secret pockets – one for toenails,
one for chocolate,
if you have a third pocket to store tissues and
squashed sultanas,
if you stuff caramels inside your shoes when you
walk to class,
if you squeeze a lollipop in your armpit and hold
your elbow tight,
if you balance a biscuit under your school hat,
if you smuggle a banana up the sleeve of your
jumper,
if you curl your fingers around a marshmallow –
one per hand,
if you sneak chips from your pencil case and
muffle the crunch with a cough,
if you use your cheese sandwich as a bookmark,
if you slurp strawberry milk through a straw
under the desk,
if you arm your underpants with popping candy,
if you are foolish enough to eat a lamington
behind a library book,

BE WARNED –
even if your teacher does not say a word,
they will have seen,
they will have heard.

Mr Farwig

Mr Farwig, yes that's his name.
He teaches Year 4,
and it would be fun to say he actually wore a wig –
– you know the sort for men, a rug
like a little tea-cosy where there used to be hair –
but he doesn't. In fact, Mr Farwig
has hair like a rooster's that scrapes the ceiling
in orange spikes and prongs.
Once I asked him a question about maths.
When he leant over, his hair got me right in the eye.
I was blinded, tears everywhere,
and he just kept on explaining the sum –
not the slightest idea of what he'd done.
And Mr Farwig has a nose like a spade.
It's flat and impressive, the sort an elf
might climb if it had ropes and proper boots.
Mr Farwig says it's not because
he used to be a boxer, but just in case
no-one likes to look him straight in the eye
and we always try to laugh at his jokes.
More than anything, though, Mr Farwig is made
of questions:
What do you think you're doing?

Did the dog eat your homework again?
Did I say to chat to the person beside you?
Who threw the paper plane?
Why are there crumbs all around your mouth?
Would you like to tell the rest of the class what's so funny?
Do you want to get up and teach?
Would you like to go for a walk to the principal's office?
Why DO you have that pencil halfway up your nose?

Test

I wish my brain
worked just the same
when I take a test.

It worked last week
and yesterday,
but something goes wrong
when I have one hour long
to prove how much I know.

I have that paper
on my desk to thank
for making me draw a blank
and perform
at less than my best.

School Sprinkler

Strange the way,
on a boiling hot day,
the cool, clear glitter
of our school sprinkler
falls exactly where
we play.

Soccer – a Story in Ten Games

The first time I played soccer
I ran so hard
I thought my head would explode.

The second time I played
my breathing was so fast
I thought I'd run out of air.

The third time
I nearly scored and I'm sure
my heart skipped a beat.

The fourth time
we *almost* scored
three times – *Aaagghhh!*

The fifth time
my team scored
and my heart really did skip a beat!

The sixth time I played
I thought, *We can't lose*,
but we did.

The seventh time
I thought, *We can't win*,
but we did!

The eighth time
I let through a ball in front of the net,
misjudged a header and earnt a headache
and missed an open goal.
I thought, *Maybe this game isn't for me*.

The ninth time I played soccer
I did all that – and more – but
we ended with a draw.

I can't wait to play again.
Bring on game number ten!

Why Can't I Whistle?

When I try to whistle
I wonder why the air
crossing from inside to out
through my pout
says nothing at all
till I'm ready to pass out.

Why is it so easy for some
with their fingers,
teeth, thumb?
When I try to whistle
my mouth just feels numb!

When you whistle, your lips and the air inside your mouth vibrate, which causes soundwaves.

Break-up Day

December,
the school year
careering toward the holidays
and cheering us on at the finish line!

Summer Lies

Summer lies –
somewhere out there
b e y o
n d t h
i s w i
n d o w

beside
the
river

n e
e a
b th
the
trees

between

the flags

and upon
the

e
z
e
e
r
b

The Flood

What was once a street
is now a swift river.

What once was a playground
is a pond for the birds.

Where there were cars and buses,
now boats and surfboards.

Where there was a hallway
lies a dark underwater room.

Where there were sounds
of the city, people laughing,

now silence, and tears.
In this flood the water delivers

many things – sirens, broken bridges,
the stench of mud, mould,

nights lit by candles and the moon,
days filled with crackling radios,

and then the sun, in boots
with brooms and hugs and brushes,

with sandwiches, salvaged memories
and strangers becoming neighbours.

Mad

I've never known my dad
to be more mad
than when he's leaning over
our broken lawnmower!

Old Men

World-weary old men –
I don't understand them.
Do they understand me –
the child they used to be?

Viewpoints

They see mess
I see lots of toys

They hear loud music
I hear happy noise

I see dirt
They see germs

They see a garden
I see worms

I see lollies
They see decay

I see a year
They see a day

I see mud
all over my shirt

They see a lot
of very hard work

I think *CLIMB*
when I see a wall

They think *CAREFUL,*
YOU MIGHT FALL

They see dusk
no more play

I see more hours
left in the day

They say *early bed*
I say *half-past nine*

They see ice cream
I see all mine!

Scary poems
and disgusting poems

What Can Fit through a Keyhole?

What can fit through a keyhole?
A secret,
a whisper,
the blink of an eye.

What can fall through the floorboards?
A coin,
a dream,
a chink of light.

What can slip through a locked door?
A ghost,
a scream,
the darkness of night.

The Tracks

What is it that steals the tracks?

Is it the wind that blows them away
so no-one will know where you walked today?

Is it the dog, its nose to the ground,
that blurs the footprints so you can't be found?

Is it the rain that washes clean
any trace of where you've been?

Is it the leaves that sweep the tracks
so you cannot find the pathway back?

Is it the silent magic of night
that removes all things created in light?

Does the bogeyman rub them away with his hand
so they are lost like grains of sand?

Do they hide with birdsong and spirits of trees
in the places that eyes cannot see?

Can they crawl through cracks and creaking chairs,
creep up behind you? *Who's there?*

Outside it's dark and the tracks have fled.
Will they find a way back to the foot of your bed?

Night-light

I always leave on the light
so the night
won't get a fright!

Sock Monster

sneaks socks
from under your nose.

It especially likes the taste
of little children's toes.

Let's hope it doesn't steal more
than one sock from each pair in the drawer.

A Ghost in the Toaster

A ghost lives in our toaster.
It never makes a sound,
but it changes the dial
with an invisible smile
so my toast turns black, not brown!

Leave the Lamp On

I need to leave the lamp on
to shed a little light
into the darkest corner
after kisses and *goodnight*

to chase shadows from the doorway
and monsters behind my bed,
so I can sleep in fields of sunshine
inside my head.

When I Am Old

for my children

When I am old and whiskered and wrinkled
when my back is curved and crooked and crinkled
when my skin is sprinkled with spots and bumps
when my tummy is full of lumps
when there's hair growing out of my ears and nose
when I've bunions and blisters on twisted toes
when the wind whistles through my missing teeth
when I creak and I clunk and collapse at the knees

I will still love you. Will you still love me?

Gross Multiple Choice

Which of these makes the most noise?

a) weevils waking up in your bowl of cereal
b) maggots wriggling through your meat pie
c) cockroaches cracking jokes in your chips

What the Cockroach May Have Said When It Lost Its Head ...

Hey, who turned out the lights?
I'd like to gobble up these crumbs, but where's my mouth?
It's suddenly quiet around here. Where did everyone go?
Help! I've lost my mind!

A cockroach can live for over a week after it loses its head.

How to Grow Mushrooms

Doesn't everybody know
what grows between your toes?

I've warned you once that in the heat
dirt collects on stinky feet.

Fat dirt worms will tend that soil
and after several days of toil

the spores are sown, then start to sprout.
If you're lucky, you'll pull a mushroom out!

You Choose

What is worse?

Stepping barefoot in doggy doo
or cleaning it out of the tread of your shoe?

The boy who picks his nose
then passes you a chip?

The girl who coughs into her hand
then pokes her finger in the dip?

Chomping on your own
or someone else's toenails?

Breathing in a fly
or swallowing a snail?

The Snakeskinned Crocodile

The Snakeskinned Crocodile is the rarest of beasts.
Imagine not one but two nightmares released,
two reptiles in a death roll, above and beneath.
Hours later when the wrestling match has ceased,
if the croc has proved its stamina the least,
it dons the serpent's scales on every bulge and
crease,
its tight new skin for living in – fit for the
victor's feast.

- -

Snakes have been known to swallow crocodiles.
It can be a major battle that takes hours for a victor to emerge.

how many noses in a nostril?

Nonsense poems and great gobbledygook

How Many Noses in a Nostril?

How many noses in a nostril?
How many hairs on a tongue?

How many tastebuds in an eyeball?
How many fingers on a thumb?

How much sun in a freckle?
How many skips in a stride?

How many brains in your belly?
How far left to go when you arrive?

Spell for a Silly Mood

A basket of beetles
A busload of bats
A pig in the pudding
A cupful of cats

A song in my sandwich
A zoo in my shoe
A truck in the treetops
A germ with the flu

A hat full of jelly
A school down the sink
A cartwheeling cream bun
An ear that can wink

Trifle

Little version of the way
I'd like the world to be:

jelly for foundations
        colourful and light
jam roll for the nations
        united in their plight
strawberries and blueberries
        to populate the plains
yellow clouds of custard
        bring comfort from the pain
and a miracle from up above –
        chocolate falls like rain.

Jellybean Rainbow

for my daughter, Sappho

Jellybean rainbow
blueberry mansion
chocolate diamond
marshmallow money

the metaphor
grows sweeter
when you double
the honey!

The Dog and the Billy Goat

after Edward Lear

A dog and a doughnut went to sea
on the back of a billy goat.
When the doughnut grew crumby,
goat moved it to his tummy.
Uh-oh – now they won't float!
Dog looked up at the stars above
and sang with a sombre note,
'O lovely Billy, O Billy, my love,
I wish you had not
        had not
        had not
I wish you had not eaten our float!'

Billy said to his pal, 'O please do not growl,
and here is another thing.
I would not have tarried
with the doughnut we carried
had I known it was our safety ring!'
They drifted away and beyond the bay
to the land where the bombie tree grows.
How the two of them cheered when a turtle
    appeared

with a net tangled round her nose,
        her nose,
        her nose,
with a net tangled round her nose.

'Dear turtle, can it be, you are tangled in debris?'
'The net,' said the turtle. 'That's right.'
So they pulled it away. 'How can I repay,'
said the turtle, 'the two of you?'
Instead of doughnuts or a boat
she gave them a magnetic spoon.
Then hand in hand, she steered them to land,
through the compass of the moon,
        the moon,
        the moon,
through the compass of the moon.

A bombie is an outcrop of coral reef that can resemble a column or a trunk of a tree growing out of the water at low tide.
Turtles use natural light, like that created by the moon and stars, to navigate the oceans. There is a theory that turtles have inbuilt 'magnets' that allow them to pinpoint their exact latitude and longitude.

The Termite Rap

A tree-load of termites moved onto my deck.
They chewed their way up the ten front steps,
then let themselves in – straight through the door.
No need for a key! No knock! No *Hello*!
Just walked with their backpacks of dusty old
  clothes
into dark little rooms underneath the floor.

They contacted friends on the termite line,
texting the message, *The wood here's divine* ☺
Those termites kept coming – they liked what
  they saw.
Five hundred families from the front fence,
great gangs of workers who had the good sense
to make the long journey from the mailbox next
  door.

They climbed in through windows, sashes and sills,
hid in the curtain flounces and frills,
widened the gaps between tongue-and-groove
  walls.
They networked roads from skirting to ceiling.
In the hallway, a highway was appearing.
That wasn't enough! The mites wanted more!

Teams in the loo rattled tiles under toes,
grinding a path to the shower rose.
The legs of the table grew thinner and thinner.
More in the bedroom wearing my clothes,
ticking like clocks right under my nose.
When I wanted to dream, they wanted their
dinner!

Restaurants in the bookshelf! Discos in the roof!
Crews of termites getting on their groove!
Joking, laughing and clapping their paws,
hip-hop rapping when the house fell silent,
drumming, tapping and dancing up a riot.
Click-clack scritch-scratch sung with rasping jaws.

Trillions of termites called our home *theirs* too.
Their gnawing – worse than snoring. There was
nothing to do
but declare to every termite THIS MEANS WAR!
Grab your dusty backpacks! I'm taking back my
home!
Text your mates, *Get out of town* ☹ I'm picking
up the phone!
Pest control's on the other end waiting for my call!

Gridlocked termites filled verandahs and railings,
leaping to freedom onto branches and palings
and woodpiles and stumps where they'd lived
before,
leaving only silence … and ghostly tracks,
walls and floors with wind and sun tarmacs.
The battle ended, but nobody won this war!

The Crocodile and the Letter 'L'

The crocodile's tongue
is stuck fast
to the bottom of its mouth.

If the crocodile could speak
it would greet you
with, *Hewwo.*
What a wovewy day!

It couldn't lick its lips
or poke out its tongue,
but if it uttered politely,
Wouwdn't you wike to stay for wunch?
I'd strongly suggest you run!

Dinosaur at West End

I'm sure I saw a dinosaur
descending on Orleigh Park.
Well, okay, it was growing dark –
but its legs were as big as the Moreton Bay fig
and its mouth was as wide as the river
and although it was a warm summer night
I couldn't help but shiver!

Just a Tickle

Some folk, when they make you wait
say, *Just a minute.*
Won't be long.
On my way now.
Almost home.

One in particular
is a desperate trick:
you may have heard it –
I'll just be a tick.

Well a clock doesn't stop
so that *tick* becomes *tock*
then *tick tock tick tock tick tock tick*
times ten, twenty, one hundred, more!

Don't be guilty of this little lie.
Counting is a wasteful way
to pass the time.
Measure the moments
in laughter, not seconds.

When you're next running late
forget, *Just a tick,*
and try, *Just a tickle!*
and offer a giggle (or two)
so we all enjoy the wait!

Twaddle

A wolf in sheep's clothing,
decoy-duck, sly boots,
ventriloquist, magician,
storm in a teacup,
poetic licence,
hocus-pocus nonsense,
bosh, tosh, drivel,
flight of fancy, extravaganzy,
wonderland and cuckooland,
castles in the sky,
the bee's knees, gibberish,
mumbo jumbo,
absurdity and truth
by ratbags, poets,
yarn tellers who say *struth,*
all in the mind's eye –
the decision rests with you.

coming to your senses

Poems about the five senses (and the other hidden ones)

Coming to Your Senses, Coming to a Poem

Listen with your ears,
not with your nose.

Speak with your mouth,
not your heels and toes.

If you're especially clever
it will come as no surprise

that to listen even better
you need to use your eyes.

If speaking with your mouth
seems somewhat bland

to say things extra-specially
you can use your hands.

A tongue is a fine instrument
to convey a taste sensation,

but you'll need a nose and eyes
for a flavour revelation

and it's no secret that a laugh
calls for open lips,

but if you want to belly-laugh
you'll need to add your hips.

A smile, too, requires a mouth,
but in order not to lie

you'll need to smile a smile
that uses both your eyes.

To touch somebody else
use fingers or a cheek,

so they feel a little more
add the words you rarely speak.

But you may feel the kindest touch
when you are alone,

when coming to your senses,
when coming to a poem.

Butter

Butter
yellow
solid
cold

Butter
burnt
black
old

Butter
melted
shiny
gold

Butter
baked
cake
sold!

Strange Little Animal

Strange little animal that lives in my mouth
Pointer to east, west, north, south

Strong ball of muscle to push and pull
Stops for a rest when the stomach says *FULL*

Sees the world through salty, sour, bitter, sweet
Too hot, too cold, just right to eat

As discerning as a finger's touch
Detects bumpy, slimy, hard, soft, rough

As stubborn with taste as a spoilt child
Loves or hates spicy and mild

So many memories within every bud
Of seasons, families, meals made with love

A host of personalities, it's often polite
But can also be silly and poke out in spite

Playful as a puppy, tickly as a feather
Sensitive to tears and all sorts of weather

A tiny acrobat, nothing it can't do
Suck, swallow, speak, lick, blow, chew

The index, middle, pinky, ring and thumb
Third hand of the body that gets jobs done

Brain Food

My custard apple
looks just like a brain
– only green!

Then again,
so does this walnut
without the skull of its shell!

Sometimes I stick peas
to mashed potato
and make a brain
with bumps and warts –
perfect for a witch or toad!

But my favourite brain
is yellow jelly
wobbling on my plate.

I take my spoon,
sculpt it to perfection,
then decorate

with hundreds and thousands.
This must be
what a brainwave looks like!

Eating with Your Eyes

for Lili Manon

Our baby girl
is learning
to feed herself.

We load her spoon
with mashed pumpkin
and hand it to her.

She smiles,
opens her mouth wide,
watches as she brings

her food up to her face,
then places her spoon
in her eye!

The Subtle Art of Satiation

Oh please, don't squeeze
too much into me.
I am only one tummy –
not two or three!

Satiation, or being 'sated', means feeling full or satisfied. It can happen when you've had a big serve of your favourite meal.

Sydney Opera House

The home
lies within the house

as does the song
within the mouth.

The dreamy swimmer
on the water:

Belief, its mother;
Beauty, its daughter.

Visualisation

Today I am going to practise piano
without lifting a finger.

The great revelation
is that visualisation
lets me practise my scales
and the most difficult pieces
all in my head
while lying in bed.

I close my eyes and get to work!

Firefly

The world sleeps,
but the bushes are waking.

Darkness blinks,
shaking off the day's light.

Fireflies ring
the silent bells of night.

Umbrella Song

for Sappho

Umbrella up
Rain drops drizzle

Umbrella down
Wind howls whistle

Umbrella up
Sun shines sizzle

Umbrella lost
Wet cold sniffle

Umbrella lost
Umbrella lost

Unsolved riddle

Party Animals

Give a possum a tin roof,
a few tall trees,
a powerline
and it can't resist!

It'll surf those waves
of corrugated iron,
tap dance
inside your ceiling,

walk the tightrope,
then miraculously,
tail coiled,
become the trapeze!

Look out! Here's one now
crashing through the stars
and it's headed
straight for your dreams!

Fuzz

I love to say this funny word.
I love to see it on a baby bird.
I love to feel it on a peach's skin
or underneath a puppy dog's chin,
but I don't like it growing inside my bin!

Fight   Flight   Freeze

If ever you are very scared
your body may do one of these:

Fight   Flight   Freeze

Adrenalin can be your friend
if you get a fright,

making your heart beat very fast,
making your muscles tight

so you can stay and use all your might
or run away – that's *Fight* or *Flight*.

And if it's too hard to do either of these,
your body may choose to simply *Freeze*,

using stillness and silence as defence.
It remains like this until danger ends.

Fight   Flight   Freeze

Swing

Funny how
just a simple thing
causes my tiny ear bones
to sing.

Vestibular sensory input is the kind of sensation you receive when you are swinging. It is detected by structures in your ear and helps you to balance.

Dance

I want my body to tell the story,
        a tale of sadness,
        a tale of glory.
Words can't always say it for me.

I'll let my body tell the story.

Squeeze Cuddle

Hug me
        Hold me
                Squeeze me tight

Cuddle close
        Grab my hand
                Everything will be all right

Boom Crash Poem
(Proprioception Poem)

Stomping on the floor,
banging on a drum,

going for a walk,
speeding to a run,

hopping on one leg,
pushing up against the wall,

clap my hands together,
bring my knees in tight,

give myself a big hug.
Now I feel just right!

Proprioception is an important sense. When your body moves and you place pressure on your muscles and joints, this helps you to know where you are in space (even with your eyes closed). It also feels great!

a pocket full of poems
Poems to keep in your pocket to feel safe and hopeful

Safe Place

I want a hidden pocket
sewn inside my shirt.
I'll place a little poem in it
and go there when I'm hurt.

Disappointment

Looking in the letterbox
every day,
finding nothing
with my name on it.

Little

Sometimes *Little* finds itself lost,
hidden down low among legs,
stuck behind the tall heads.

Little's voice may not be heard,
swallowed up by a crowd
or a big and a loud.

Sometimes *Little* tries not to be seen,
especially when *Little*
attracts bossy or mean.

But *Little* must see
with more than its eyes
and learn that height is just a disguise.

The Days

The days are long and wide
when you spend them all inside.

The hours are still and slow
if you have nowhere to go.

The minutes are massive and stick like glue
when there is nothing you must do.

The seconds are heavy and bury you deep,
you feel as if you are asleep

if you don't see a single soul,
if you lose your lovely goal.

I Want a Best Friend

I want a best friend
who will sit beside me,
happy to say nothing or chat all day.

I want a best friend
who lets me disagree
and knows that we don't have to be the same.

I want a best friend
who's happy to compare clothes, hair, lunches,
hopes and grades,
but in the end, doesn't care.

I want a best friend
who's there, even when they're not, who lives
overseas or interstate or down the road,
who's normally early or often late, but always
has time for me.

I want a best friend
who likes me when I'm sad or spotty or sick,
when I don't get picked for the team,
when I don't get the joke or an invitation to the
party.

I want a best friend
who forgives me when I'm wrong,
who sticks around when everyone has gone.

I want a best friend
who wants the world for me,
who likes me when I'm just *me.*

That's the best friend I hope I can be.

Beauty

Pretty might look perfect
and cute as any button,

but beauty is another thing
and only comes from loving.

Half Full

Glass half empty.
Glass half full.

Halfway up
or down the hill.

Your best is better
than half-hearted.

Begin! Begin!

You're halfway there
just because you started!

Seeing things as 'half full' and always hoping for the best is called being optimistic, whereas seeing things as 'half empty' and taking the gloomiest view is called being pessimistic.

Hope

hope
walks
up the
back
steps
quietly
so no-one
will
notice
it has
a little
song
clenched
in its
fist

Release Your Wish

I wish, I wish
for more than this.

It's time

to dance the scary dance,
to sing the first goodbye.

I can see the little strings
lowered from the sky.

I'll grab hold and climb,
I'll try.

What Are Wings For?

for my father, Ross Taylor

To thread a song through the eye of the tree
To utter a breath when you cannot breathe
To shelter fear, so it may sleep

To follow the footsteps of children and stars
To share the sky with those behind bars
To call home dreams that strayed too far

To speak the words that can't be spoken
of seasons, sunsets and windows thrown open
To find the new nest, to mend what is broken

High

little bird
    high up
        and helmetless

tiny tufts
    of hope
        throat full of sky

bravery has no eyes
    it just pulls
        like gravity

it knows your name –
    it's calling
        calling to you

fly   fly   fly

A Poem Is a Good Place

A poem is a good place
to store a laugh,
right between nonsense and noses,
toilets and toes,
behind buckteeth and bottoms
all seated in rows,
slap-bang in the middle
of silliness and your soul,
a good place to return to
so you don't grow old!

What Will You See?

Darkness falling
or the first star,

the dying flames
or the glowing embers,

a wrinkled face
or a twinkle in the eye,

the times you failed
or the times you tried,

the years in your life
or the life in your years,

that you are lonely
or perhaps alone,

that you are lost
or the world is your home,

that you are unique
or you don't belong,

that feelings are weak
or make you strong?

What will you see –

all you are not
or all you'll become?

I Love You All the Days

after Sappho

I love you all the days
and all the dark nights.

I love you all the way home
and all the way back again.

I love you all the great oceans
and all the small ones too.

I love you all the forests of trees
and all the stars strung above these.

I love you all the deserts and flowers,
all the droughts and winter showers.

I love you in so many ways;
I love you all the days.

Goodnights

I can't get enough *goodnights*,
each one a little rope
the day lets down
gently, lowering me
into the stars below.

What to Do with Worries

for Scotia

I know a girl
who gets a fright
when the lamp goes off
and there's no light.

Here's a few words
she could try
to make her worries
feel all right.

Wait a moment,
close your eyes,
take a breath,
smile a smile.

Dream a dream
of a special place,
stay a while
where you're safe.

Let each worry
board a boat,
growing smaller
as they float.

Away, away,
out of sight.
Sleep is your friend
and so is the night.

Sleep Softly Sweetly Safely Sound

The wind was wondering what to wear
all around and about the air,
it tumbled treetop to trunk, trunk to treetop,
lapped the leaves and the light poles,
looped the loops of clothes lines.

To flap and lift, unfurl and fly
with towels and sheets, socks and dresses
across open skies
and swimming pools, the school, the shops,
the showground, the sleeping streets,
along the shoreline, the sand and shells,
away from land and out to sea.

Up, up through the shadows
toward matter and magic,
toward tonight, tomorrow, today,
caught on the tides and the moon,
the fabric for the stars' room,
to dress the dreamer and the bed,
to rest the heart and the head.

I Wish for You

for my dear readers

I wish for you a pillow
full of popcorn, wobbly teeth and bunk beds,
wagging tails, pogo sticks, somersaults and
magic tricks.

I wish for you a coat
stitched with spaghetti and chocolate buttons,
treasure hunts, disco dances, water bombs and
second chances.

I wish for you a blanket
made of midnight movies and tall stories, hugs
and moonlight, big dippers and snow fights.

I wish for you a necklace
threaded with bubblegum, comets and monkey
bars, tree houses and coins in jars.

I wish for you a book
of bare feet and tippy-toes, bellybuttons and
burps, laughter until it hurts, hundreds of
wonderful people and yet to be written,
unimaginable sequels.

Author's Note

I can't thank you enough for taking the time to read these poems.

Some adults think poetry, especially nonsense poetry, is too small and silly to mean much. I disagree – but I am a poet, so I'm biased. It's better that you are the judge of that – of what you like and don't like. Just remember, it's not always the adults' fault. Just as some people are afraid of flying, some people are a little afraid of poetry. This is where you can help. By sharing your favourite poems, you help others understand that poetry isn't meant to be scary.

I've called this collection of poems *100 Ways to Fly.* I hope you don't feel cheated if you read this entire collection and are still unable to fly. My title uses metaphor – *to fly* or *take flight* – and is one way to think of poetry. Sometimes the small group of words crafted into a poem can unexpectedly lift you up, take you away somewhere wonderful and bring you safely home again after you've experienced a whole new view of the world.

It's amazing to think that a poem can change a moment, a day and occasionally even a life. I hope you will find many more ways to fly … with poetry!

Answers to the Seven Riddles

One: Pillow

Two: Balloon

Three: Banana

Four: Picture frame

Five: Poem

Six: Sunburn

Seven: Echo

Acknowledgements

I would like to thank the Australia Council for the Arts for a literary grant to support the writing of this collection, my daughter, Lili Manon Taylor, for assistance with editing, and my family for coming along on the ride with your belief, your love and your wild imaginations! I want to thank my publisher Kristina Schulz for believing for so long that this book could take off, and my editors Mark MacLeod and Felicity Dunning for generously honing the punctuation and potential of each poem.